The Hit-Away Kid

by Matt Christopher

Illustrated by George Ulrich

Little, Brown and Company

Boston   New York   London

To Stephanie Owens Lurie

Text copyright © 1988 by Matthew F. Christopher
Illustrations copyright © 1988 by Little, Brown
and Company (Inc.)

First Paperback Edition

The characters and events portrayed in this book are
fictitious. Any similarity to real persons, living or
dead, is coincidental and not intended by the author.

Library of Congress Cataloging-in-Publication Data

Christopher, Matt.
    The hit-away kid / by Matt Christopher. — 1st ed.
    p.   cm. — (A Springboard book)
    Summary: Barry McGee, hit-away batter for the Peach Street
Mudders, enjoys winning so much that he has a tendency to bend
the rules; then the dirty tactics of the pitcher on a rival team give
him a new perspective on sports ethics.
    HC: ISBN 0-316-13995-5
    PB: ISBN 0-316-14007-4
    [1. Baseball — Fiction.   2. Conduct of life — Fiction.]   I. Title.
PZ7.C458Hi 1988
[E] — dc19   87-24406
                                                        CIP
                                                         AC

Springboard Books and design is a registered trademark
of Little, Brown and Company (Inc.).

        HC: 10 9 8 7 6 5 4
        PB: 12 11

                COM-MO

Printed in the United States of America

The Hit-Away Kid

1

It was the top of the fourth inning and Barry McGee, left fielder for the Peach Street Mudders, was bored. He loved baseball, and he loved to win. He would do almost *anything* to win. But today's game was slow as molasses. A ball hadn't been hit out to him since the first inning, when the Belk's Junk Shop batters had knocked out seven hits and racked up six runs. It sure had looked as if they would *never* get out.

Then the Mudders had scored three times

in the second inning and once in the third, proving to the Junk Shoppers that they were still in the game.

But now Barry felt as if he were just one of the spectators. The Shoppers were hitting the ball in every direction but left field.

Crack! Barry reacted to the sharp sound of the bat connecting with the ball and saw the white pill zip past pitcher Sparrow Fisher's head. Center fielder José Mendez scooped it up and whipped it in to second baseman Nicky Chong, holding the Belk's Joe Tuttle to a single.

Maybe good ol' Brian Feinberg will pop one out to me, Barry thought hopefully.

Good ol' Brian popped one out, all right, but it was to right fielder Alfie Maples.

Then Eddie Lathan hit a hard one to shortstop Bus Mercer, who had to go to his right a little to catch the ball. But he flubbed it. And by the time he had control of it, Joe was on second and Eddie was on first.

"That's okay, Bus!" Barry yelled, knowing how Bus must feel after making an error. He hated making errors, too. Nothing was worse, except maybe striking out with runners on base.

Sparrow mowed Monk Solomon down with three straight strikes, bringing up the Belk's left fielder, Jerry Moon. Jerry was a right-hander, but he batted from the left side of the plate. No way, Barry thought, will he hit a ball out to me.

Crack! Jerry belted Sparrow's first pitch to deep left field. Surprised, Barry turned and sprinted toward the sign-covered fence. A hit would score a run. A catch would end the inning. He glanced back over his shoulder, saw the ball dropping down fast over his head, and reached out for it.

Just then he tripped over a lump of sod. He lost his balance and started to fall. But he kept his eye on the ball and got his glove under it just as he hit the ground.

It was a great play . . . until the ball rolled off his glove and onto the grass! In a flash Barry retrieved it. His back was to the umpire and the crowd — who could see what he did? He jumped to his feet, shouting, "I've got it! I've got it!"

"Out!" yelled the base umpire.

Barry ran in, holding the ball up in his gloved hand and grinning widely. He heard some Peach Street Mudders fans yell, "Nice catch, Barry!"

Then another voice from the sideline said, "You dropped it. I saw you."

2

Barry's smile faded and his heart leaped as he glanced toward the sideline. There sat his sister, Susan, and their little brother, Tommy. Barry had seen them there earlier but had practically forgotten about them.

He gave Susan a dirty look that said Keep your mouth shut. Then he turned away and continued on toward the dugout.

But some of the Belk's Junk Shop fans must have seen him drop the ball, too. "He dropped it, ump! What are you, blind?" a couple of them yelled.

Luckily, the umpire's decision held. Jerry Moon was out.

So much for your big mouth, Susan, he thought. But at the same time, deep down he felt guilty. What he'd done wasn't right. Well, he'd have to forget it, that's all. If he could.

Sparrow, batting last in the lineup, led off with a single. Then Barry stepped to the plate. He felt comfortable here. He'd rather bat than field any day. Maybe, he thought, he could get a long hit and make up for his cover-up.

He glanced at Coach Parker, who was coaching third base, and got the bunt signal.

Barry couldn't believe it.

"Oh, no!" he moaned. "I can't bunt!"

He decided he wouldn't bunt, no matter what the coach had signaled him to do. Even though he was leadoff hitter for the Mudders, he was known by a lot of the players and fans as a hit-away batter, and he liked that. It made him feel good. Important.

Anyway, so far today he had gotten a single and a walk. He deserved to keep swinging. Maybe this time he could sock the old apple out of the lot for a two-run homer. He was due for a round-tripper.

Barry stepped into the box, waited for the first pitch, and shifted into a bunting position. He missed the pitch deliberately. He missed the second one, too, even though both pitches were almost directly over the heart of the plate.

Then he looked at the coach again and saw him give the hit-away sign. Barry hid a grin. I fooled him, he thought.

He didn't hit a round-tripper, but he managed to lace a line drive between third base and shortstop for a single.

"That-away, hit-away!" a fan yelled.

Barry smiled.

"Tell me something, Barry," Monk, the Belk's first baseman, said. "Did you really catch that fly ball?"

Barry stared at him. "Of course I did!" he snapped. He let his eyes bore into Monk's dark ones for a moment, then he leaned over to tuck his blue socks under his white pant-legs. He hated to lie. But it was too late to tell the truth now. Like his father used to say when such situations came up, Never trouble trouble till trouble troubles you.

Turtleneck Jones — who got his nickname from the turtleneck sweaters he usually wore — batted next and drove a double between left and center fields. Sparrow scored, and Barry circled the bases to third.

Coach Parker approached Barry from the coaching box. His eyes were shadowed by the baseball cap pushed low over his forehead. "Barry, who do you think you're kidding?" the coach said sharply. "You missed bunting those balls on purpose. You were lucky to get a hit, but the next time I give you a bunt sign, you bunt. Understand?"

Barry blushed. So he *hadn't* fooled him.

Silent, he nodded.

"Okay. Play it safe," Coach Parker cautioned. "Make sure the ball goes through the infield before you run for home."

The coach returned to the coaching box, and Barry turned his attention back to the batter, his best friend, José Mendez. José took a called strike, then popped out to short for the first out, bringing up T.V. Adams. T.V. was short, stocky, and *smart,* and he could hit the ball a mile — if he connected. Barry remembered that T.V. had doubled in the second inning and flied out in the third. As a cleanup hitter, he's due for another long hit, Barry thought.

He glanced back over his shoulder at the scoreboard. Junk Shop 6, Mudders 5.

A hit could score two runs, putting the Mudders ahead, Barry reflected. But suppose T.V. didn't get a hit? Suppose he popped up, or hit a grounder . . . ?

"Keep on your toes," Coach Parker's soft

voice reached him. "If he hits it, make sure it goes through."

"Strike two!" cried the umpire, as Finky O'Dell, the Junk Shop's left-handed pitcher, steamed his second pitch past T.V.

Oh, no! Barry thought. What's T.V. going to do? Strike out?

Then . . . *crack!* A sharp grounder down toward first base! T.V. dropped his bat and scooted for first. And Barry, seeing that the ball *seemed* to be heading past Monk's right side, bolted for home.

"Barry! Wait up!" Barry heard the coach yell.

But he was several running steps away from third base by now, too late to turn around and go back. Monk was diving after the ball, which was between him and the bag, and Barry thought, *I should be able to make it. And we need this run to tie the score.*

3

"Hit the dirt! Hit it!" cried Bus, standing beside the plate with a bat in his hand.

Barry's cap had already blown off halfway down the basepath, and he was puffing like a steam engine as he raced for home, where Brian Feinberg was waiting for the throw-in from first base. Barry hit the dirt just as Brian caught the ball. Barry tried to slide around him, but Brian had the plate covered like an umbrella.

"Out!" yelled the ump.

Barry sat there a minute, looking up at the ump, then at Brian, and finally toward first base, where Monk was poking a fist into the air in triumph.

"Nice play, Monk!" a Junk Shop fan yelled.

Monk got T.V. out, then threw me out, Barry realized. It sure *was* a good play.

He rose to his feet, brushed the dust off his white uniform, and ran to get his glove and cap off the roof of the dugout. As he headed for third base, he almost collided with Coach Parker.

"Hold it, speedy," the coach snapped.

Barry froze. That voice meant business.

"Don't tell me that you didn't hear me yell at you to wait on third," the coach said firmly. "I yelled it loud enough for the whole crowd to hear me."

"Yes, I heard you," Barry admitted, glancing briefly at the coach. His dark, angry eyes sent shivers through him. "I'm sorry. I . . . I thought I had a good enough lead."

"You *thought*. Listen, you're no different from the other players, Barry. You play by the same rules as everybody else. So let me do most of the thinking here, okay?"

Barry nodded, embarrassed. Lowering his eyes, he started to trot out to left field.

"Hold it," the coach said. "After all that running, you need to sit for a while." He glanced toward the dugout. "Tootsie! Take left!" the coach ordered.

A short, stout kid sitting near the middle of the dugout cried, "Yippee!" Then, pulling a glove onto his left hand and tugging at his cap with his right, he ran to the outfield. He flashed a smile as he passed by Barry, but Barry didn't see it. He was heading, head bowed, toward the dugout.

"Jack, take short." He heard the coach snap another order.

Jack Livingston, a tall, thin redhead, ran out to replace Bus at shortstop. All at once Barry didn't feel so bad. The coach was putting in other substitutes, too.

Barry could still hear the coach's strong words ringing in his ears. He sure knows how to drill them into a guy, he thought. But was the coach 100 percent right? I *almost* scored, Barry said to himself. I wonder what the coach would've said if I'd been safe? He probably would have clapped like crazy.

"You play by the same rules as everybody

else," the coach had said. Barry remembered the fly ball he had dropped and retrieved in time to fool everybody. Well, almost everybody. Why did Susan have to be sitting in that particular spot on the sideline, anyway? Now he'd think about that play every time he saw her. And he saw her a lot.

"Hey, man, can't wait till we play you guys next week." A strong, husky voice broke into his thoughts.

Barry turned to see a kid peeking around the edge of the dugout. A kid whose face was more familiar than any other pitcher's in the Summer Baseball Junior League.

"Why?" Barry asked Alec Frost, the High Street Bunkers' fastball pitcher.

"Why?" Alec laughed. "Because you haven't struck out yet. And that's what I'm going to do. I'm going to strike you out so bad the fans will forget they ever called you the hit-away kid."

4

"Deeper! Deeper!"

Barry looked up and saw T.V. Adams motioning Tootsie Malone to back up toward the fence. T.V. did that a lot. He seemed to have a real knack for predicting where the opposing batters were going to hit the ball.

As usual, he was right on the button. Arnie Nobles, the Junk Shop's leadoff batter, had blasted a home run his first time up, and it looked as if he was ready to do it again. He was a tall kid and had a lot of power in his swing.

Crack! He connected a two-two pitch for a long drive toward deep left field, just as T.V. had figured he might. If Tootsie hadn't played deep, the ball would have gone over his head for at least a triple. But Tootsie only had to take two steps back, raise his gloved hand, and catch it.

Neither team scored again. The game went to Belk's Junk Shoppers, 6 to 5.

"Well, it made no difference anyway," Susan said as she and Tommy walked home with Barry.

"What made no difference?" Barry asked.

"That you missed the ball," she said. "We lost anyway."

He glared at her. "Will you stop saying that?" he snapped. "You weren't there; I was.

And the ump called the guy out. That's it."

"I saw you drop it," Susan said evenly. "And I know you like to cheat."

"I do not!" he almost shouted. "Why do you say that?"

"Because it's true," Susan said. "Whenever we play board games, you —"

"Okay, okay!" Barry cut her off short. "Maybe I do cheat sometimes, but not all the time. And I don't do it to hurt anybody."

"Maybe not. But you hate to lose," Susan argued. "And if you can cheat a little, and make up your own rules —"

"You sound like Coach Parker," Barry interrupted her again. He tried not to let her arguments get under his skin, but he couldn't help it. "He said something to me about making up my own rules, too. What's wrong with liking to win, anyway? Everybody likes to win, don't they?"

"Yes. But not by cheating."

His face burned. *Cheating.* He was really beginning to hate that word. "Just don't say anything about it to Mom and Dad," he said gruffly. "I don't want them jumping on my back, too."

Susan shrugged. "Okay by me. It's your problem, not mine."

Barry looked at her a long minute. He thought he'd feel better after she said that, but he didn't. He felt worse.

At dinner, Barry's father didn't lose any time asking about the game. "How'd it come out?" he wanted to know.

"They lost!" Tommy yelled.

Everyone laughed. Tommy didn't talk a lot, but whenever he did he made a point.

"You're pretty quiet, Barry," Mr. McGee observed. "Didn't you get any hits?"

"Two singles and a walk," he answered.

"Great!" His father beamed.

"And I made a tough catch," Barry went on. He thought he could feel Susan's eyes on him, but she was calmly eating. Suddenly Barry didn't have much of an appetite.

"Well, that's good work, son," Mr. McGee said proudly.

"There's more. I dropped it . . . ," Barry confessed. "But I pretended I didn't."

5

Barry's parents stared at him. "You *what?*" his mother exclaimed.

Barry's heart pounded. "I pretended I caught the ball," he said.

Susan cleared her throat, and Barry looked at her. Their eyes locked, and he wished she could read his mind: *Keep out of this, little sister.*

"And you got away with it?" his father said and shook his head. "Barry, I'm surprised at you."

"And I'm disappointed," his mother added,

her eyes wide as she looked at him. "What a terrible thing to do, Barry. I think you should tell Coach Parker."

"It's too late for that, Mom," Barry said. "I'm sorry I did it. Okay? I promise I won't do it again."

Susan coughed, and their eyes clinched again.

"I said I won't, and I won't," he said to her, his voice higher. "Okay?"

"Okay!" Susan cried. "I didn't say a word, did I?"

"No, but you coughed," he said. "That's almost like saying something."

"Okay, okay," Mr. McGee cut in to settle the argument. "Barry apologized for what he did, and I'm sure he won't let it happen again. Now let's finish our dinner."

Barry breathed a sigh of relief. Boy! he thought. What a big deal over a stupid dropped ball!

*   *   *

The next morning Barry felt like skateboarding with José. Just as he lifted his green-and-white skateboard out of the closet, he heard his sister's high-pitched voice ask, "Can I skateboard with you? I won't be in your way, I promise."

He looked at her, and then at Tommy, who was clinging onto Susan's blue jeans.

"Aw, Susan," Barry moaned. "You're always butting in."

"Butting in? I didn't butt in at the dinner table last night, did I?" she said with a gleam in her eye. "You cooked your own goose."

Barry had to smile. "Well, all right," he said. "But Tommy stays here." He leaned over and tickled his little brother's chin. "Keep an eye on Mom, pal. Okay?"

Tommy nodded. "Okay."

Smiling triumphantly, Susan pulled out her red-and-white skateboard — which was just a few inches shorter than Barry's and had a

T-handlebar — and followed Barry out the door.

Once outside, they skateboarded up the cement walk. Their wheels clacked over the cracks, and more than once Susan's board rolled off the walk.

The second time Susan bent down to put her board back on the walk, Barry noticed something blue sticking out of her left-hand pocket. That sister of mine, he thought. Her pockets are always bulging with some kind of junk.

"Hey, Barry!" he heard a familiar voice say, and he saw his friend José sweeping around the corner on his fancy skateboard.

"José!" Barry called. "Race you down the block!"

"You're on!" José replied. The two of them stood side by side for a second, then took off down the sidewalk, leaving Susan staring after them.

Suddenly four more boys on skateboards

appeared from the other direction.

"Well, look who we've run into!" Alec Frost cried. "McGee and Mendez! The Mudders outfield!"

"Not quite," said Barry, feeling a tightness in his stomach. The last guy he wanted to come across was Smart-Alec Frost. Barry recognized the other three, too. They were all members of the High Street Bunkers baseball team: Fuzzy McCormick, Judd Koles, and Tony Workman.

Both Barry and José slowed down, moving to the right side of the curb to let Alec and his friends pass by. The four boys took their time and hogged most of the sidewalk. Another six inches and Barry and José would have been on the grass.

"Hah!" Barry heard one of the guys laugh, but he ignored him. He was just glad they were leaving.

Barry and José got into position to continue their race. Then Barry heard a scream behind him. The boys pulled up short, looked back, and saw Susan yanking out her pockets and yelling, "It's gone! It's gone!"

6

Barry and José skateboarded as fast as they could up to Susan. Tears shone in her eyes and streamed down her cheeks.

"What's gone?" Barry asked.

"Tommy's figurine!" Susan exclaimed. "The little dog statue I had in my pocket! He bought it at Disneyland with his own money!"

Barry pursed his lips. So that was what was sticking out of her pocket, he thought. "Maybe it fell out while you were skateboarding," he said.

He and José helped her search the sidewalk and the ground. Suddenly he heard loud laughter up ahead.

"Look," José said. "I think the statue's been found."

Barry looked up the sidewalk. Alec Frost was rocking back and forth on his skateboard and tossing something in the air: Tommy's glass dog. His pals were laughing as they rocked and spun on their skateboards.

"That's my brother Tommy's!" Susan yelled, running toward them. "Give it back to me!"

"Bring it back!" Barry cried, running after her.

"Better watch out," Alec taunted as he teetered on his skateboard. "I might drop it."

"Come on, Alec," Barry coaxed. "Hand it over."

But Alec and his friends only laughed and took off down the street.

"Hey! Where do you think you're taking that?" Barry shouted. He sped after them, one foot on the skateboard, the other pumping the sidewalk furiously. He could hear José following him closely and Susan lagging farther behind.

What was she doing with that dog figurine anyway? he thought angrily. Why didn't she leave it at home where it belongs?

"Alec!" he yelled. "You're *stealing* that statue! You hear me? It doesn't belong to you! It's my brother's!"

"Crook!" Susan screamed from far behind him.

Alec whipped his skateboard around and stopped. His eyes bore into Barry's as Barry reached him.

"Crook? What a gas!" he said, and laughed. "Tell your sister about that fly ball you pretended you caught, McGee. Or maybe she already knows about it. If I'm a crook, what does that make you?"

"Knock it off, Alec," José said.

"Forget that," Barry said, and extended his hand. "Hand me back my brother's statuette."

"No way!" Fuzzy McCormick cut in. "Let's go, Alec! It's yours now!"

He headed up the sidewalk, one foot on the skateboard, the other pumping away like mad.

Alec scooted around on his skateboard and started to follow him. Barry stared after him, anger flushing his cheeks. It was obvious that Alec wasn't going to return Tommy's glass dog. Something else had to be done.

"Alec, wait!" he shouted. "I've got an idea!"

7

Alec slowed down, stopped, and looked back over his shoulder at him. "Yeah?" he said. "What kind of idea?"

Barry took a deep breath and let it out before he went on, his heart pounding. "Let's make a deal," he suggested, eyeing Alec closely. "If I get one hit off you, you give back the dog. Deal?"

"Deal?" Alec echoed. "They call you the hit-away kid, don't they?"

Fuzzy laughed. "They won't after the game,"

he said and started to skateboard away. "Come on, Alec. Let's go. Forget him."

"No, wait," Alec said without taking his eyes off Barry. "Sure, I'll give you a chance to get this toy back, *if* it's your brother's."

"It is!" Susan shouted.

"But you'll have to hit two home runs," Alec said, ignoring Susan.

Barry stared at him. "Two home runs? You crazy? Who do you think I am, some big leaguer?"

"The hit-away kid," Tony Workman said, smiling from one side of his mouth.

"Right," Alec said. "And, if I strike you out *twice,* I keep it."

"And if I strike out twice and get two home runs besides?" Barry countered. "What then?"

Alec shook his head. "A real dreamer, aren't you?" he said.

He started to turn away, but Barry swept up in front of him. "You're not giving me a fair chance, Alec. In the first place, that toy doesn't belong to you."

"Sure it does. And you made a great catch yesterday. Out of my way, mudface," Alec said. He shot past Barry up the sidewalk with Fuzzy, Tony, and Dick trailing after him. A few seconds later they vanished around the next block, screaming like hyenas.

"I'm going to tell Mom," Susan said, her voice ready to break. "She'll get it back."

"No, you won't," said Barry, his face shiny with sweat from the encounter with Alec. "I don't want Alec to think he's a better pitcher than I am a batter. I'm going through with the deal."

"All you care about is your dumb game!" Susan wailed.

"You just don't understand," said Barry.

"You'll have to practice more," José broke in quietly.

Barry looked at his friend. He and José had been close all their lives. But suddenly a frightening thought occurred to him. Had the awful things Alec said about him changed José's feelings? Were they still as good friends as they ever were?

"Will you pitch to me?" he said, looking hopefully into José's dark eyes.

José grinned. "Of course I will!" he cried.

They agreed to meet at the ballpark after they went home to get their equipment. Susan came along, too, to make sure Barry practiced hard. She didn't want to go home (to Tommy) empty-handed after the game.

Barry stood in front of the backstop screen, taking warmup swings with his bat, while José stood in the worn patch of grass between home plate and the pitcher's box. Susan ran out to left field, where Barry usually hit the ball.

There were five kids playing tag, all of whom Barry knew. Before Barry hit out three balls,

all five of them quit playing tag and began helping Susan field the balls.

A good feeling swelled inside of Barry as he saw one ball and then another sail over the left-field fence. But most of the hits were shallow drives over the infield, and there were a few grounders.

"Ha, ha, ha!"

He heard the laughter coming from behind him and signaled for José to hold up his next pitch while he looked around.

Standing behind the screen was Alec, on his skateboard. This time only Fuzzy was with him.

"You got the idea, hit-away," Alec said, grinning. "Practice, practice, practice. But it'll take more than that for you to win back your precious little doggie!"

8

Barry hated to see Friday afternoon come. It was the day of the game with the High Street Bunkers — the day he had to hit two home runs off Alec Frost or avoid striking out twice. Otherwise, good-bye glass dog.

What terrible odds Alec had given him! I seldom strike out, Barry thought, but I've never hit two home runs in a game in my life!

Another terrible thing was that he couldn't even pretend he was sick and stay home. He *had* to play.

Dressed in his blue uniform, his glove stuck in front of his pants, he walked with Susan to the ballpark. Neither one of them said more than three or four words all the way. It was windy, and Barry had to pull his cap down tight to make sure it wouldn't blow off.

Both teams took their batting practice, then fielding practice, and, at exactly four-thirty, the game began. The Peach Street Mudders had first bats, and Barry, as usual, led off.

He saw that smirk on Alec's face and wished he could wipe it clean off with one hot drive right at him. Or maybe one hot long one over the left-field fence.

Alec breezed the first one by him for a called strike. Then he steamed in two pitches that just missed the outside corner. Two balls, one strike.

Alec paused, then steamed in another pitch. "Ball three!" bellowed the ump.

Barry stepped out of the box for a moment, feeling good. Maybe Alec will walk me, he

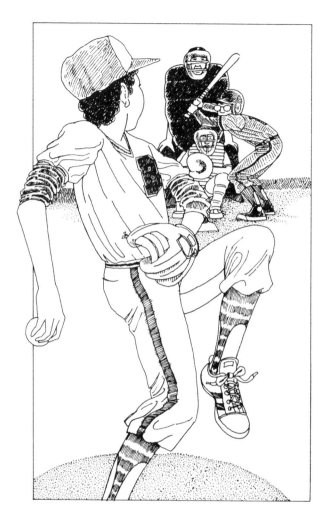

thought. At least it won't be a strikeout.

Alex pitched. "Strike two!" cried the ump.

Barry took a deep breath. He really had to watch this next pitch. It came in. Barry swung. *Whiff!*

"You're out!" shouted the ump.

Barry walked out of the box, feeling sick. One more strikeout and he — and Tommy — would never see that dog figurine again.

Turtleneck singled, and José got on by virtue of an error. Then T.V. flied out, and Randy struck out to end the top of the first inning.

Barry picked up his glove and ran out to left field, pulling his cap down tight again to keep the wind from blowing it off. It was blowing from right to left, an advantage for a left-handed hitter because the wind would tend to keep his ball in fair territory, a disadvantage for a right-handed hitter because the wind might blow it foul.

Only Tony Workman, the Bunkers' third batter, and Alec, batting cleanup, got on base, but neither could score during the bottom of that inning.

Nicky Chong led off for the Mudders in the top of the second inning and flied out to center. Barry stepped out of the dugout, put on his helmet, and leisurely picked up his bat as he waited for Alfie to take his batting turn.

Alfie struck out. Oh, man, Barry thought. Alec's on a roll today. He's already got three strikeouts, including me.

Left-hander Zero Ford, the Mudders' pitcher, lined Alec's second pitch between first and second for a single, and Barry stepped into the batting box. Again he saw that smirk on Alec's face, but he tried to ignore it. Just pitch it to me, Smart-Alec, he thought.

Alec did. "Strike one!" cried the ump.

In came another. "Strike two!"

Barry's heart pounded. He stepped out of the box, tapped the end of the bat a couple of times against the plate, then stepped in again.

Alec pitched. It looked like another strike.

Barry swung. *Crack!* The ball left his bat and zoomed out between left and center field. Deep . . . deep . . . deep . . .

9

HOME RUN!

Barry almost knew it would be the moment he hit it. He carried the bat halfway down the baseline before he tossed it aside and ran around the bases. He heard the fans yelling and could hardly resist the temptation to turn and look at Alec and see the expression on his face.

But he didn't look. He didn't have to. He had gotten what he needed. A home run. All he needed was one more. But it's not that easy, pal, he told himself. He'll pitch differently to you the next time. He might even strike you out. You're still in deep trouble no matter how you look at it.

The cheers stopped after the guys slapped fives with Barry and he sat down near the end of the dugout. Zero, who had also scored, sat beside him. Then Susan came and sat on his other side, giving him a big smile. "That was beautiful," she praised him.

"Thanks," he said. She was nice to him, but he knew she'd never forget the fly he had missed in last week's game.

Turtleneck doubled, putting him in a position for another run. But José struck out on a two-two pitch, ending the top half of the inning and giving Alec his fourth strikeout. He's really hot today, Barry thought worriedly as he picked up his glove and trotted out to left field.

Dick Strom, leading off for the Bunkers, drove a hot liner between Turtleneck and

Sammy that went for two bases. Barry fielded the ball and whipped it to third to keep Dick from running there. Then Judd singled, driving in Dick.

"Close to the foul line, Barry!" T.V. yelled at him, motioning him over as Dave Apple came to the plate.

Dave blasted a long fly to deep left that went foul by inches, but Barry caught it for an out. Good ol' T.V.! Barry thought.

Zero walked Jake Jacoby, and Fuzzy popped a fly to short. Then Ron Bush walked, and Tony grounded out to shortstop for the third out. Mudders 2, Bunkers 1.

Only Bus managed to get on base in the top of the third inning, and that was because of an error by the shortstop. Then Alec led off for the Bunkers and lambasted Zero's first pitch for a homer over the center-field fence. It was, Barry thought, probably the longest hit he'd ever seen there.

Andy Campbell kept it rolling by cracking

out a single. Dick walked. Judd popped up. Then Dave doubled to right center field, scoring two more runs. Zero fanned Jake for his first strikeout but walked Fuzzy. Ron singled over short, scoring the Bunkers' fourth run. Then Tony laced a grounder to Bus, which Bus fielded for the third out. Mudders 2, Bunkers 5.

They're really rolling, Barry thought, still worried as he and the rest of the Mudders trotted off the field to start the top half of the fourth inning. Alfie hit a hard one down to shortstop, which Fuzzy missed. Then Zero singled over short for his second hit, sending Alfie to second.

And Barry came up.

"Barry!" called the coach.

Oh, no! Barry thought as he glanced down toward the third-base coaching box. He's not going to take me out, is he?

"Look those pitches over carefully," Coach Parker advised, clapping his hands softly.

Barry nodded, took a deep, relieved breath, then stepped into the batter's box. The first pitch was slightly low and inside. Barry let it go by.

"Strike!" said the ump.

Barry and the tall guy in the white pants and shirt exchanged looks. Then Barry got ready for the next pitch. It came steaming down the middle of the plate, and Barry swung.

Crack! A shallow drive to deep left center field!

Barry dropped the bat, raced to first . . . to second . . . to third . . .

He missed touching second base, but he couldn't stop now. He kept going.

10

Barry saw Coach Parker holding up his hands as he came running in to third base, and he stopped there, breathing hard and sweating. He took off his helmet and cap and wiped the sweat off his forehead. Then he looked directly at the coach and nervously wondered, Did he see me miss second base? Did the umpire see me?

The coach was smiling. "Nice hit, Barry," he said.

"Thanks," said Barry. "But I . . ." He faltered. *But I missed second base!* he wanted to say. *And no one saw me! I could get away with it, just like I got away with it the time I missed that fly ball! But I can't do that again! I won't do it again! I wouldn't be any better than Alec if I did!*

He saw that Jake, the Bunkers' third baseman, still had the ball, which had been thrown to him from left field. Calmly, Barry stepped off the bag.

"Barry, watch it!" shouted Coach Parker. But Barry showed no reaction that he had heard. Jake jumped toward him and tagged him out.

"Barry! Didn't you know he had the ball?" the coach demanded.

Barry nodded. "Yes, Coach. But I hadn't touched second base," he said honestly, and loud enough for some of the crowd to hear him. "I figured I should be out, anyway."

The coach stared at him, his mouth popping open. But no words came out.

José slammed a triple before the half-inning was over, and T.V. knocked him in, giving the Mudders one more run. They kept the Bunkers scoreless during the bottom half of the fourth, then came to bat in the top of the fifth with the score tied, Mudders 5, Bunkers 5. Barry worried about what he was going to do the next time he went to the plate.

Randy led off with a sharp single over Alec's head. Then Nicky, after fouling off three successive pitches, flied out to center.

"Come on, Alfie," Barry said as he stepped out of the dugout and picked up his bat. "Knock him in!"

Alfie walked.

Then Zero hit a steaming hot grounder down to third that looked like a sure out, but Jake bobbled it and all the runners were safe. The bases were loaded and Barry was the next batter.

He stepped up to the plate, his heart thumping. He could think of nothing but winning that figurine back from Alec. If Alec struck him out, it was over. If he knocked a home run, Tommy would get his figurine back. But knocking a home run was like asking for a trip to the moon. He'd had one home run already. Expecting to get two of them was too much to expect.

"Strike!" said the ump as Alec blazed in an inside, corner-touching pitch.

Then, "Ball!"

Barry stepped out of the box, rubbed his hands up and down on the handle of the bat, and stepped in again.

"Strike two!" boomed the ump as another inside, corner-touching pitch steamed in.

Barry's heart pounded. He waited for the next pitch. In it came. It was almost in the same spot as the last pitch. He swung. *Crack!* The ball sailed out to deep left field! But the wind caught it! It was curving . . . curving . . . !

"Foul ball!" yelled the ump.

"Oh, no!" groaned the fans.

Barry was sick. It was so close!

He popped up the next pitch. Three outs.

It was over — now Barry would never get Tommy's toy dog back.

Turtleneck struck out, and that was it. No one scored.

The Bunkers came up for their last bats, got two men on, then scored both when Judd Koles lambasted a triple to left center field. The Bunkers won, 7 to 5.

Barry headed off the field immediately, not even wanting to see that smirking look on Alec's face, or that disappointed look on Susan's.

"Barry! Wait up!"

He turned at the sound of the voice and saw Alec running toward him. When Alec reached him, Barry couldn't hide his frustration. "What do you want?"

Alec suddenly seemed nervous. He stuck his hands in his pockets and said, "Uh, I just

wanted to say you played a good game."

"Not good enough," Barry muttered.

"You know, I've been thinking," Alec said, as he drew something out of his pocket. "What do I want with this thing, anyway?" He held out the figurine. "Here," he said, glancing briefly at Susan, then back at Barry. "It's yours. You won it fair and square. I have to hand it to you for telling the coach you missed second base. And if it wasn't for that wind blowing your ball foul, it would have been a home run easily. Here, take it."

Hardly believing his ears, Barry accepted the figurine from Alec and handed it to Susan. Then he stared at Alec, who had already turned and was running back toward his team.

"I guess he's more honest than we thought he was," Susan said.

Barry nodded. "I guess a person can change, if he does the right thing — can't he?" he said softly.

"Sure, he can," Susan said, winking at Barry. "And a person can get in trouble if she doesn't get this doggie back to her little brother real soon."

"Right! Let's go!" said Barry, and they raced each other all the way home.